SPORT-O-RAMA

Benoit Tardif

Kids Can Press

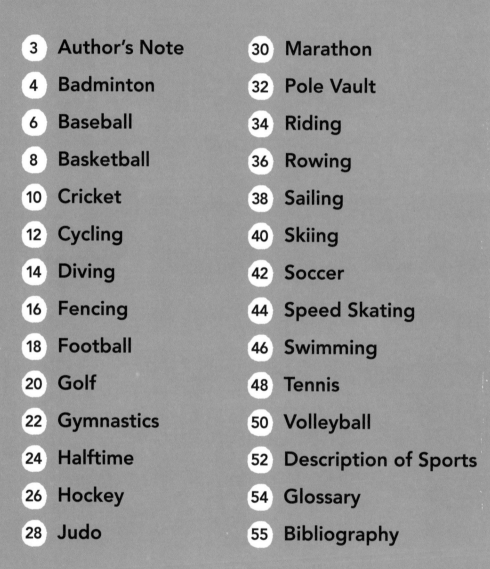

TARDIF

I've always loved sports. When I was a boy, I skied and played basketball. I was even a star hockey goalie!

Today, my work as an illustrator leaves less time for sports. But I still love settling in to watch a good hockey game on TV, a pencil in one hand and the remote control in the other.

I hope that this book inspires you to lace up your running shoes or skates, or strap on your skis and have fun!

BENOIT

BADMINTON

plastic
feathers

new birdie

real
goose
feathers

old birdie

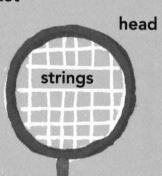

racket

head

strings

shaft

handle

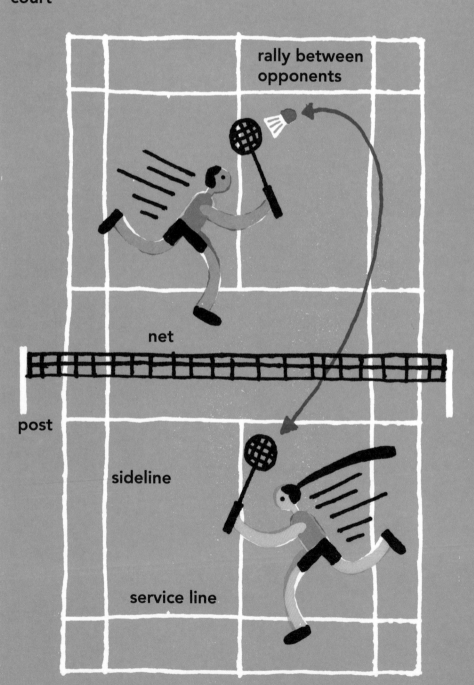

court

rally between
opponents

net

post

sideline

service line

server

SERVICE

serve position

receiver

birdie

smash

jump

protective
eyewear

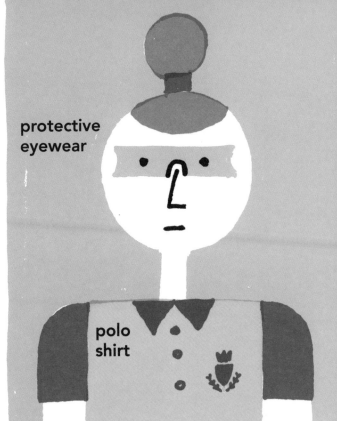

polo
shirt

knee pads

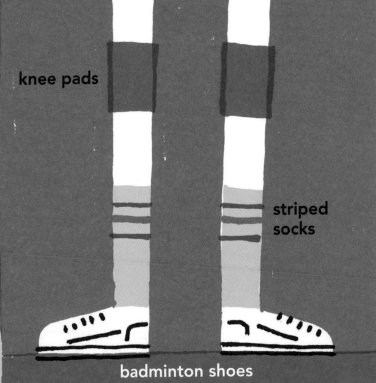

striped
socks

badminton shoes

BASEBALL

baseball

hit

YEAH!

batter

CRACK!

strike

AWWW!

WHOOSH!

baseball bat

baseball glove

thumb

handle

barrel

pocket

knob

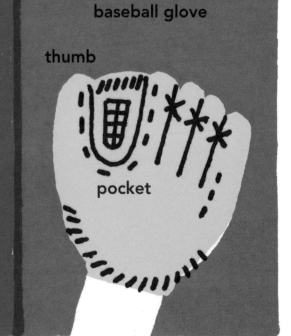

6

BASKETBALL

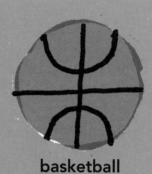
basketball

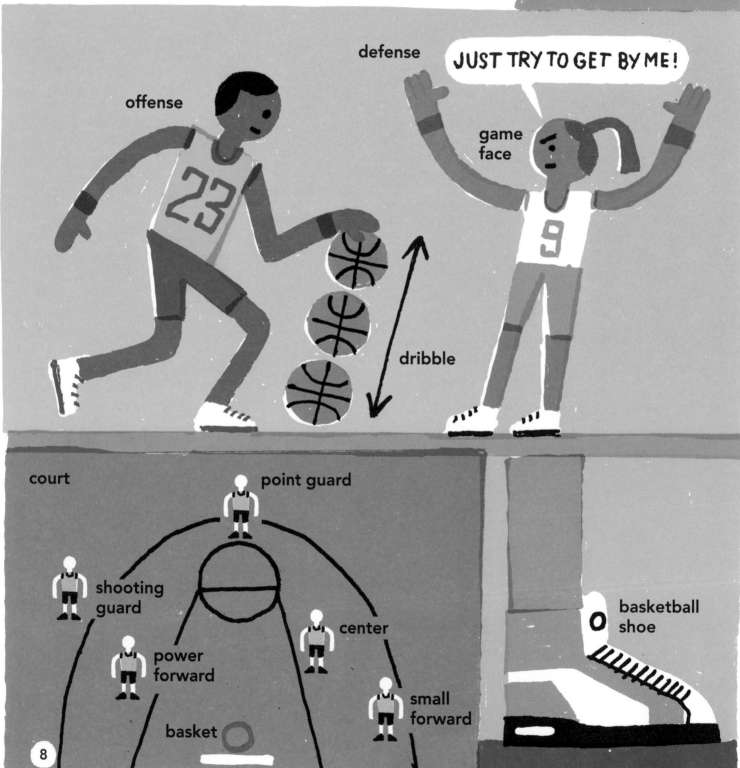

clouds

backboard

very, very tall player

dunk

headband

jersey

hoop

basket

BEAVERS

16

net

wrist-
bands

powerless
defense

shorts

referee

whistle

FOUL ON NUMBER 16!

CRICKET

cricket ball

wicketkeeper

NICE HIT!

batter in action

bat

blade

handle

10

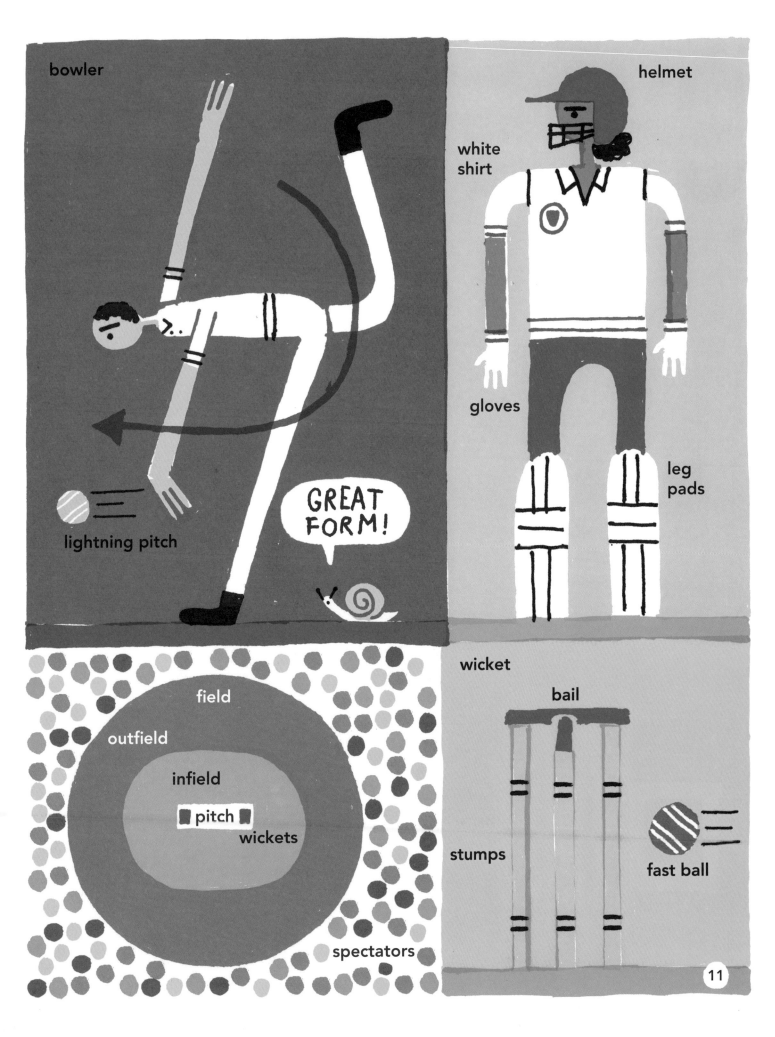

CYCLING

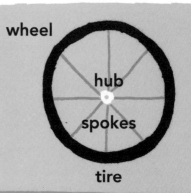

hub

spokes

tire

road racing course

HERE I COME!

very steep slope

crankset

crank

pedal

peloton

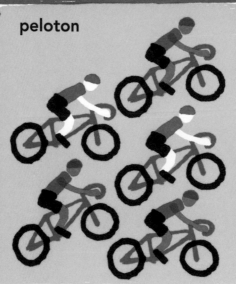

cycling glove

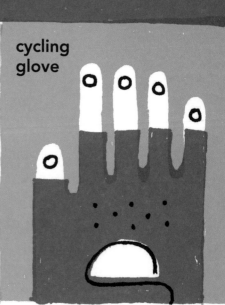

12

DIVING

medalist

tower

10 m

7.5 m

5 m

bathing suit

WHAT A VIEW!

pool

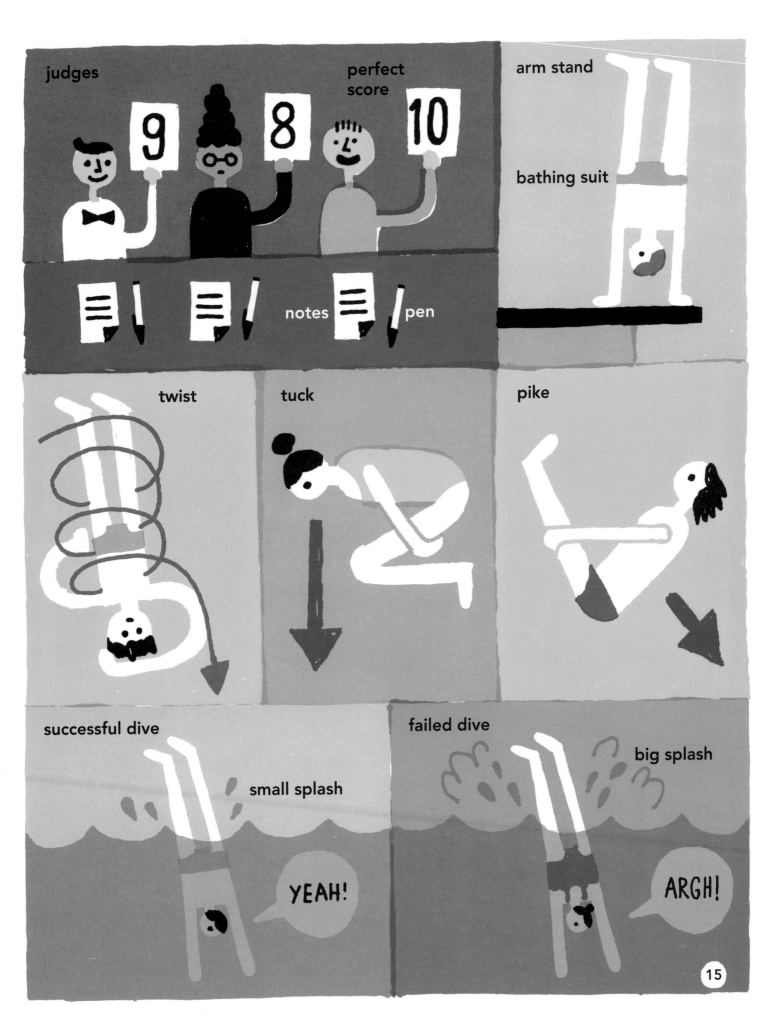

FENCING

glove

cuff

assault

EN GARDE!

mask

protective glove

metal plastron

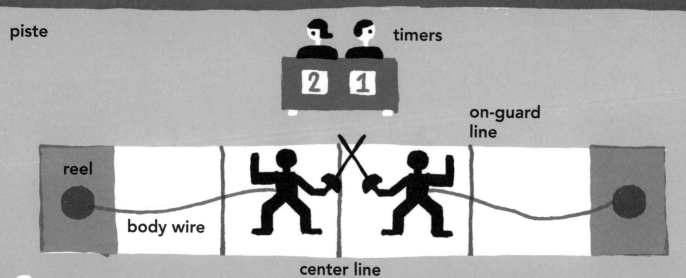

piste

timers

2 1

on-guard line

reel

body wire

center line

16

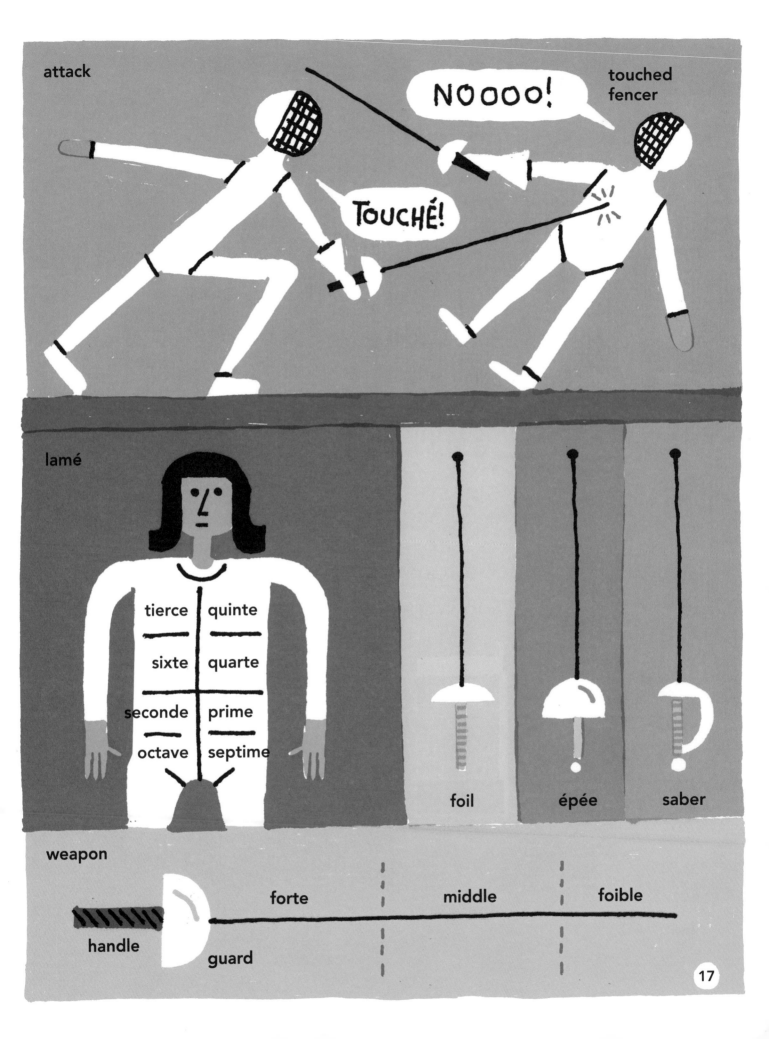

FOOTBALL

football

halfback

linebackers

MOVE IT!

NO!

NO WAY!

coach

headset

field

end zone

players' bench

10 20 30 40 50 40 30 20 10

10 20 30 40 50 40 30 20 10

goal

halfway line

18

GOLF

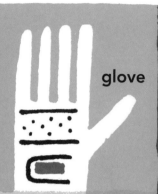

glove

golf ball

tee

golf cart

tired player

green

hole

sand trap

fairway

pond

seagull

teeing ground

golf bag

caddie

golfer

21

GYMNASTICS

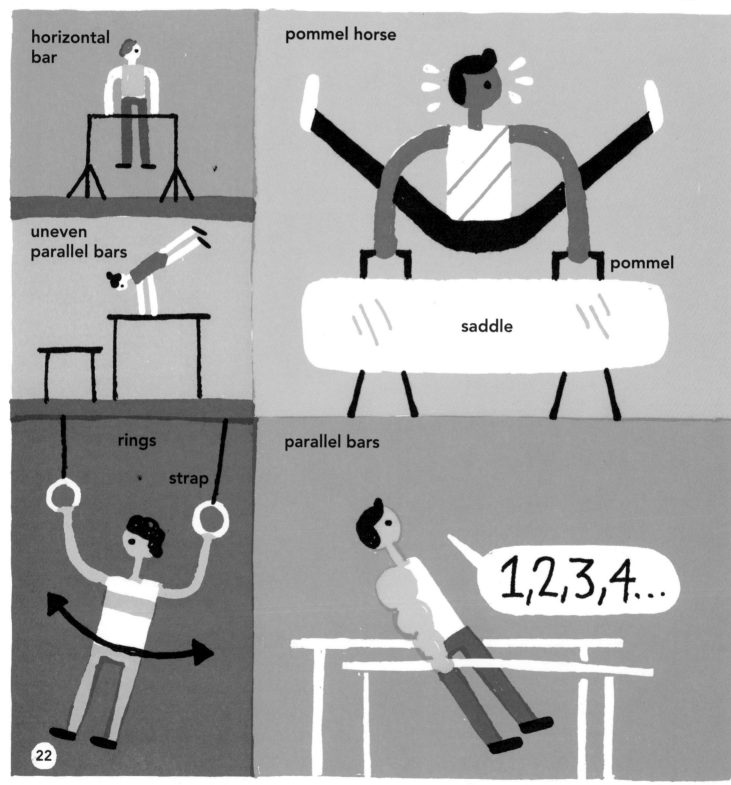

horizontal bar

pommel horse

uneven parallel bars

pommel

saddle

rings

strap

parallel bars

1,2,3,4...

HOCKEY

puck

face-off

captain

referee

determined player

stick

ice rink

handle

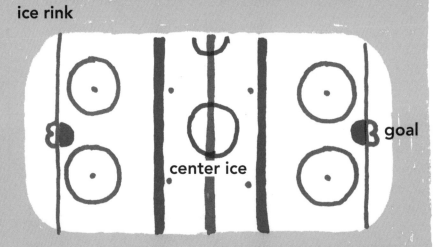

goal

blade

center ice

heel

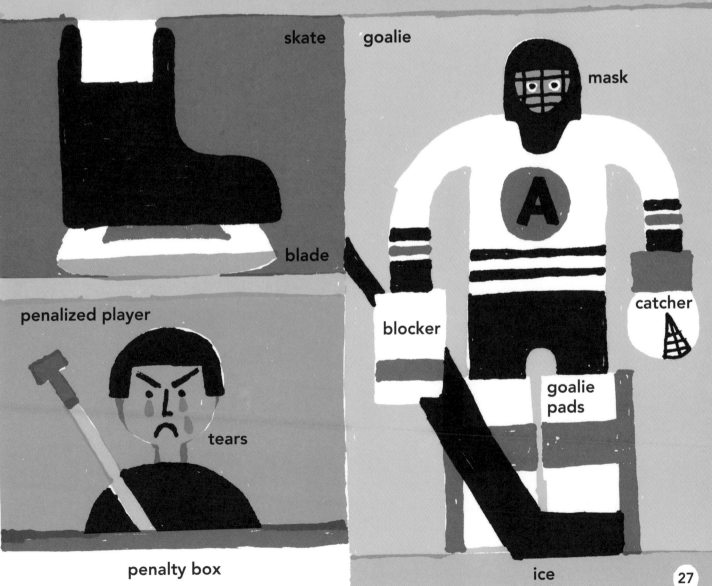

JUDO

HAJIME!

green belt

judoka

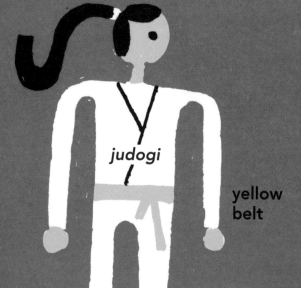

judogi

yellow belt

kumi kata

blue belt

immobilization

orange belt

immobilized opponent

*ippon
seoi nage*

brown
belt

circle throw

red belt

arm lock

black
belt

OH, NO!
NOT AGAIN!

timer   scoreboard

referee

tatami mat

corner judge

MARATHON

start signal

runners

0351

5613

9122 bib

shorts

running
shoes

bridge

spectators

GO! GO!

GO!

30

fish

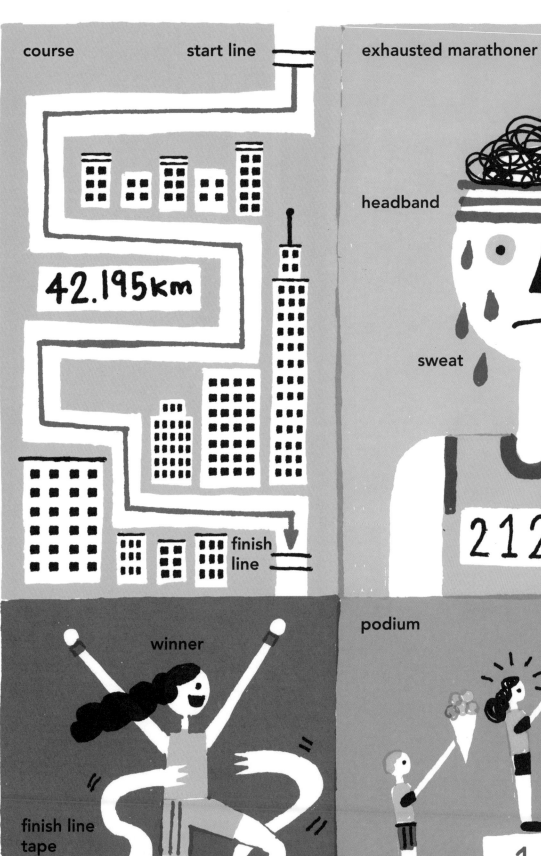

course

start line

42.195km

finish line

exhausted marathoner

headband

sweat

jersey

2121

winner

finish line tape

podium

flowers

1

2

3

POLE VAULT

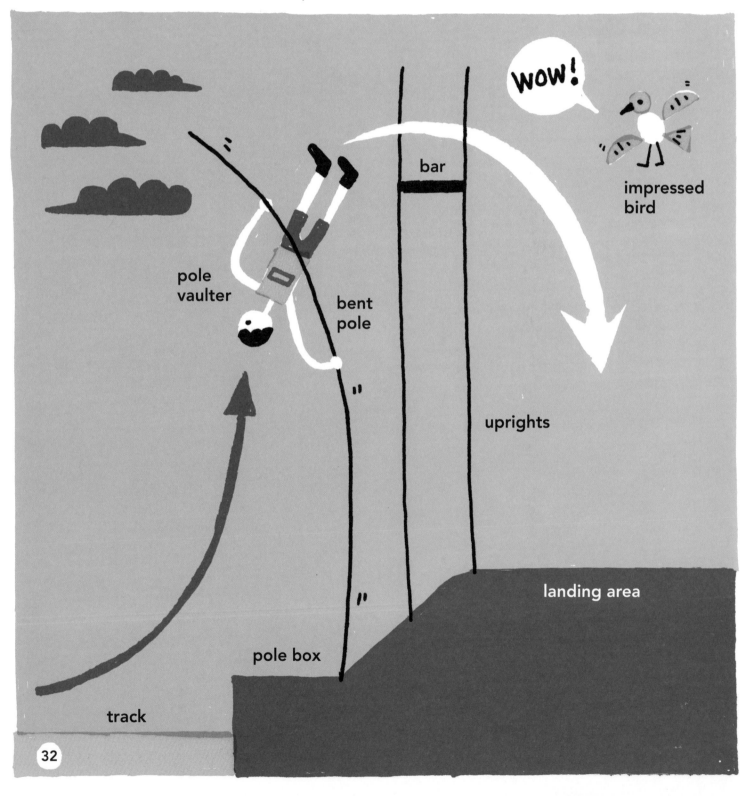

wow!

impressed bird

bar

pole vaulter

bent pole

uprights

track

pole box

landing area

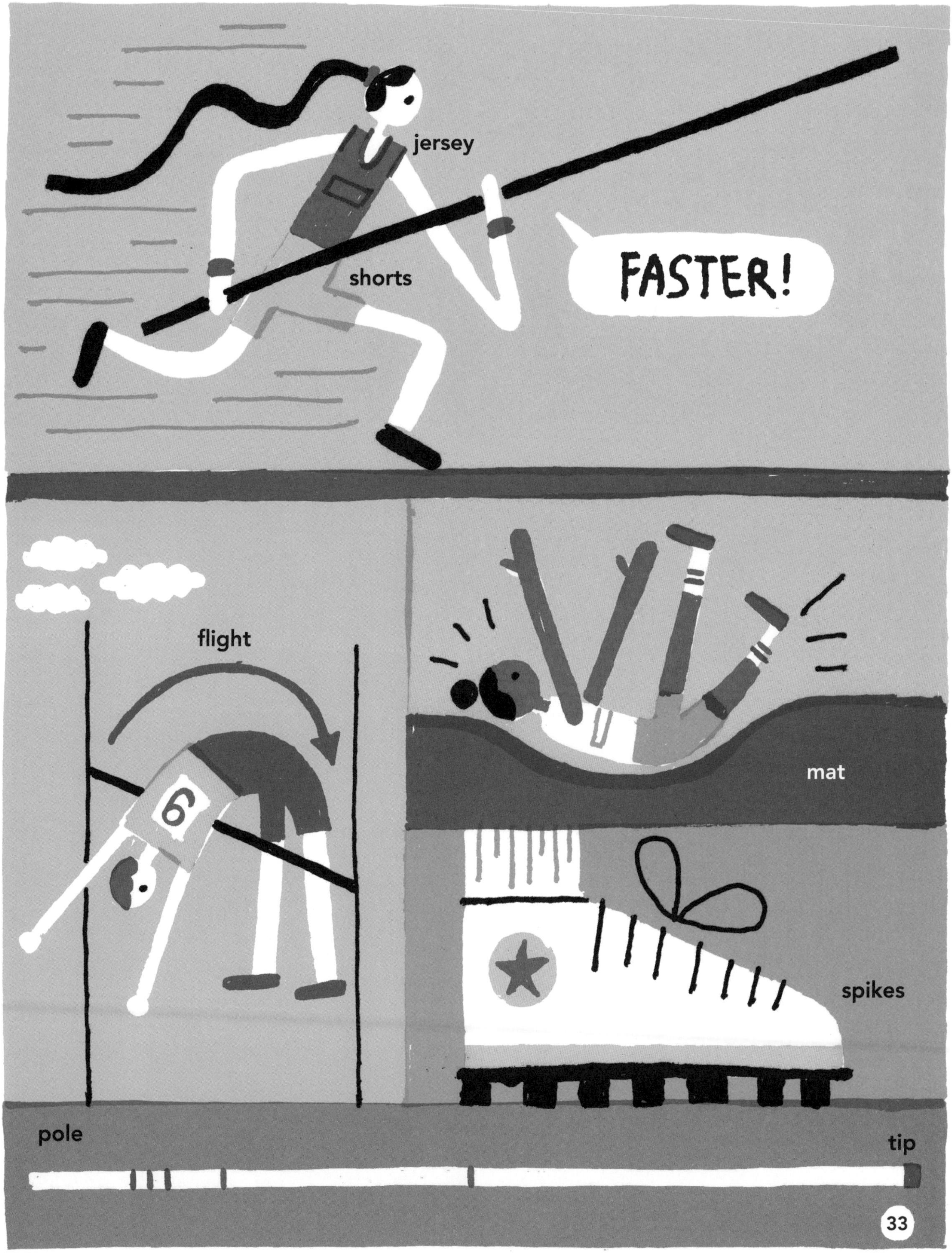
jersey
FASTER!
shorts
flight
6
mat
spikes
pole
tip

RIDING

1st prize

#1

rider

glove

UP!

riding boot

fence

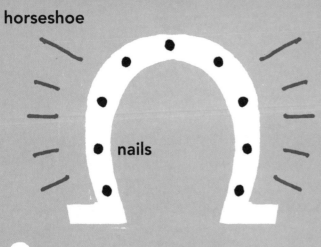

horseshoe

nails

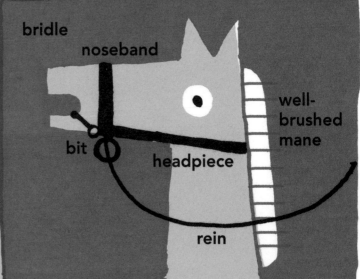

bridle

noseband

bit

headpiece

well-brushed mane

rein

34

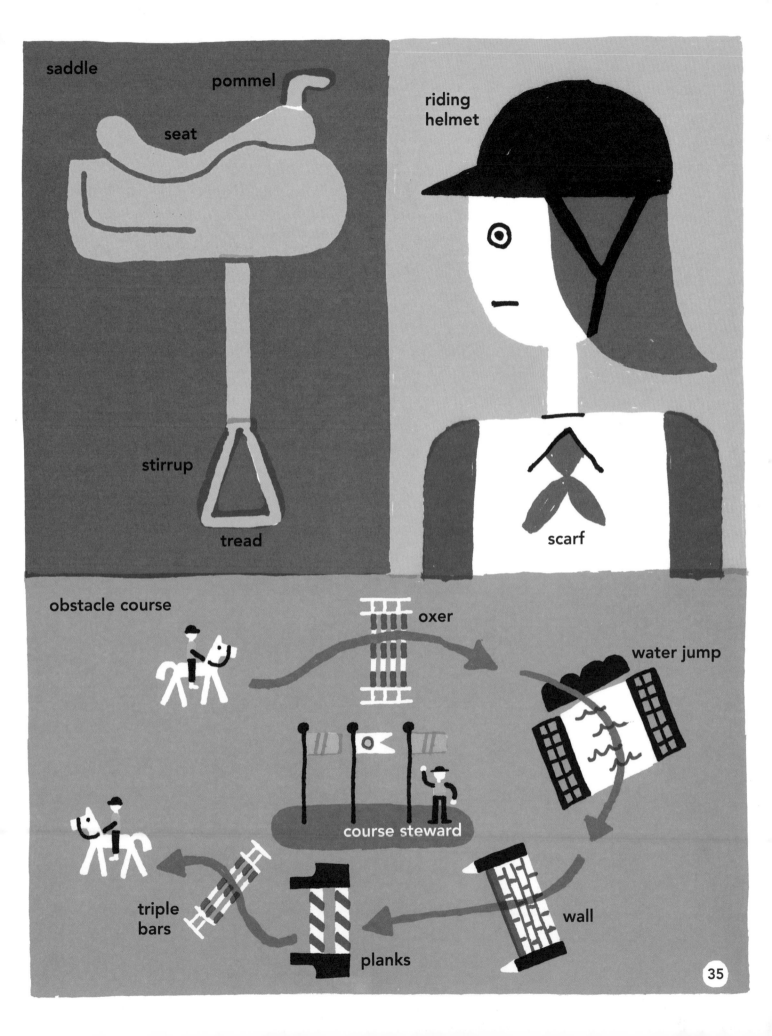

saddle

pommel

seat

stirrup

tread

riding helmet

scarf

obstacle course

oxer

water jump

course steward

triple bars

planks

wall

ROWING

four-person scull

sun

albatross

NICE AND STEADY!

shell

two-person scull

river

oar

handle

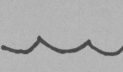

blade

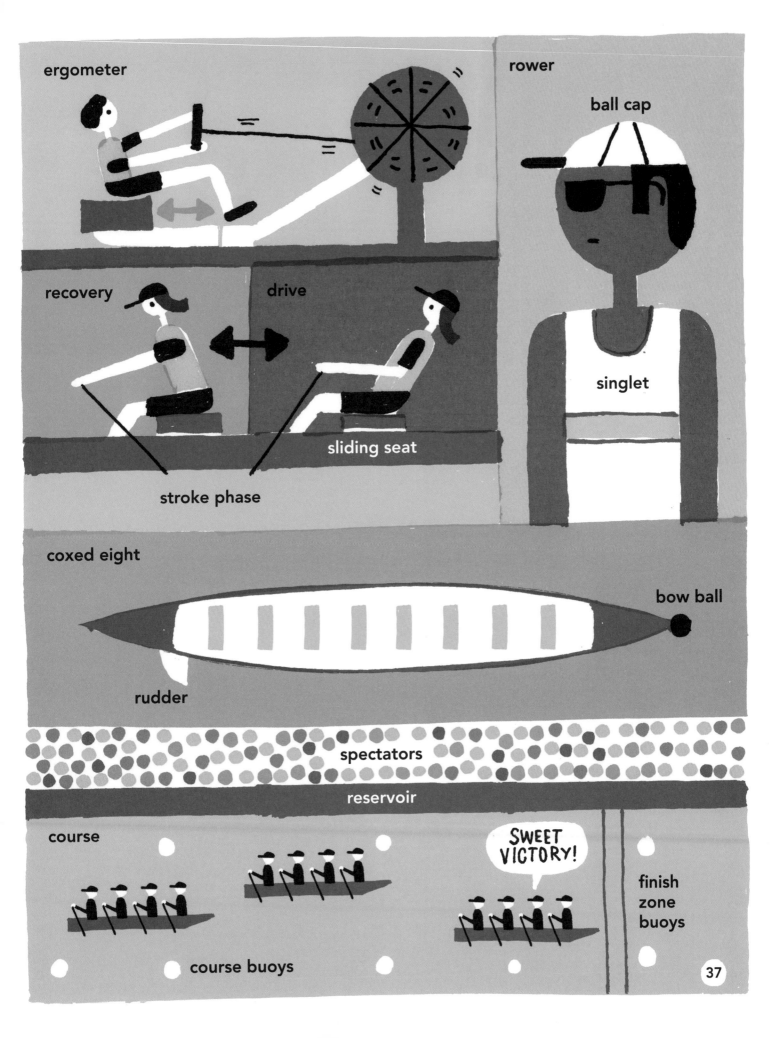

SAILING

knot

carabiner

winch

sailboat

weather vane

mast

mainsail

jib

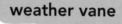

boom

skipper

cleat

tiller

hull

Lucie 4

rudder

keel

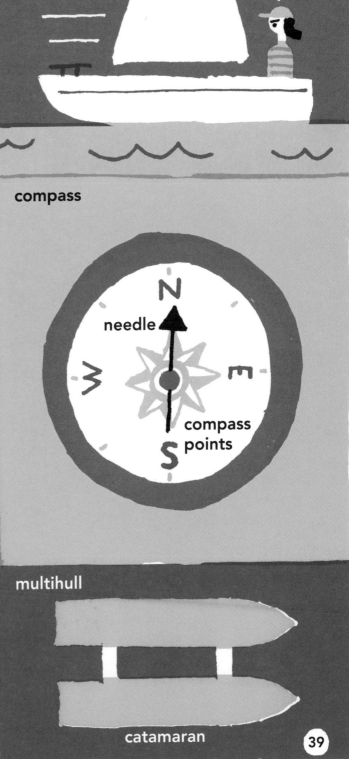

39

SKIING

ski lift

stopwatch

giant slalom

gate

FASTER THAN THE WIND!

ski poles

snow

tight bend

skis

tip

bindings

tail

ski boot

buckle

shell

downhill

WHEE!

steep slope

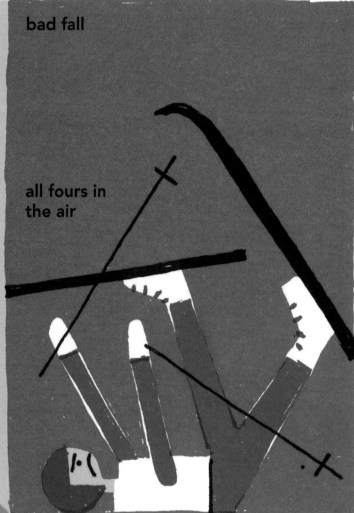

bad fall

all fours in the air

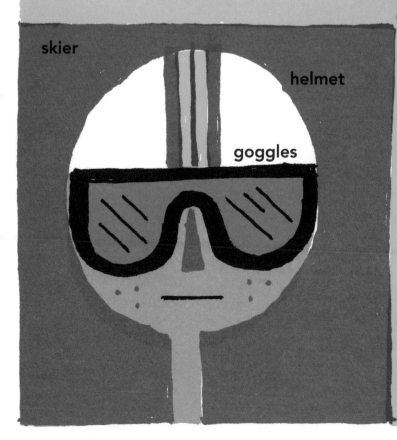

skier

helmet

goggles

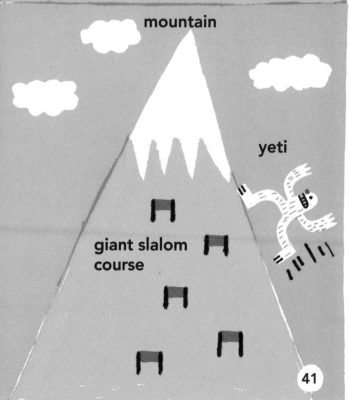

mountain

yeti

giant slalom course

41

SOCCER

soccer ball

players in action

THAT BALL IS MINE!

tackle attempt

jersey

shin guards

field

assistant referee

sock

goal

center circle

penalty area

corner flag

cleats

SPEED SKATING

skaters in action

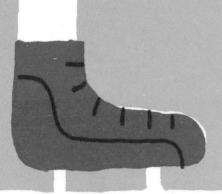

speed skate

blade

CATCH ME IF YOU CAN!

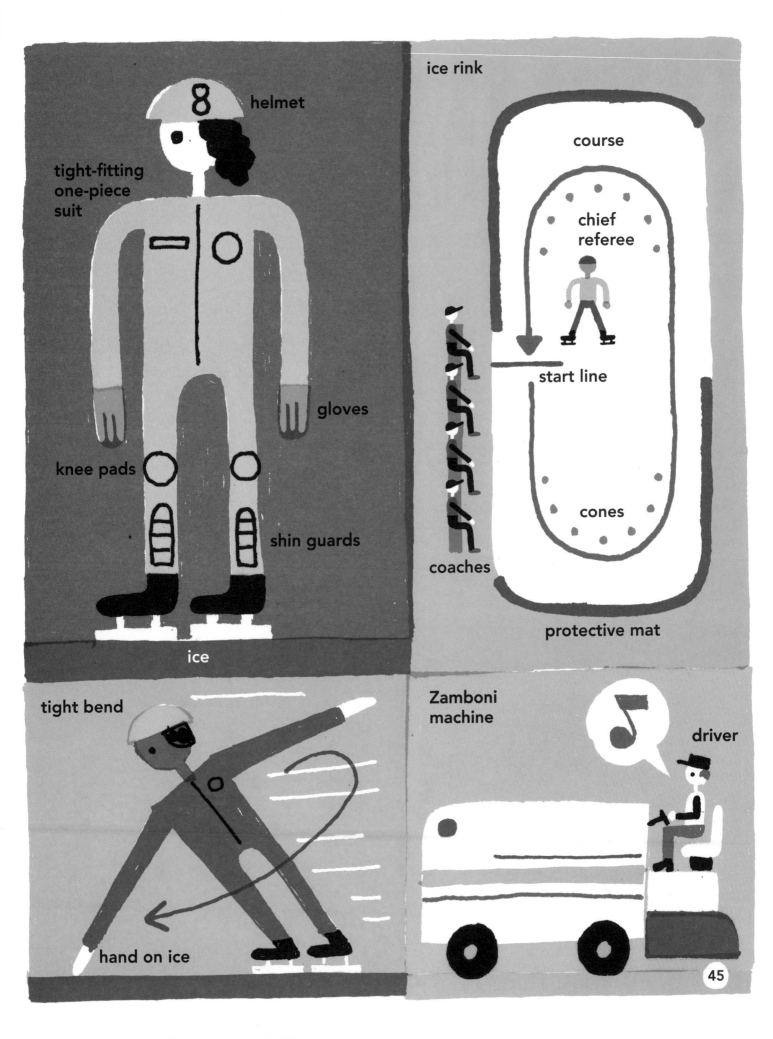

SWIMMING

ON YOUR MARKS...

starting block

water

dive

GO!

bathing suit

swimming cap

goggles

pace clock

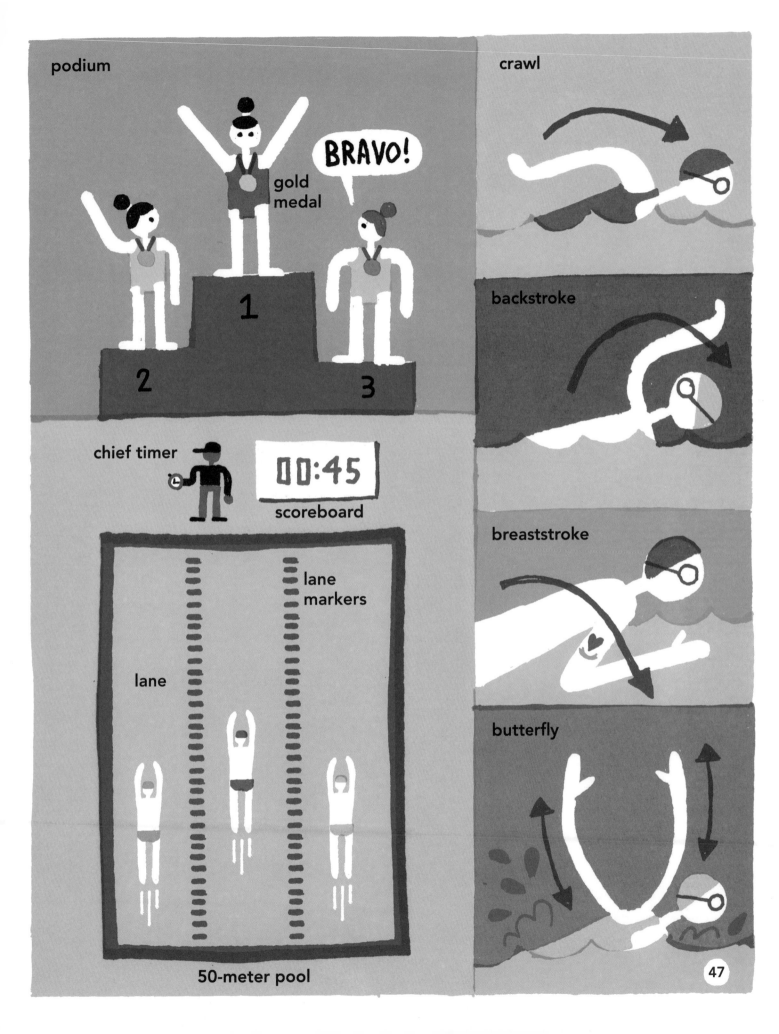

podium

BRAVO!

gold medal

1

2

3

chief timer

00:45

scoreboard

lane markers

lane

50-meter pool

crawl

backstroke

breaststroke

butterfly

47

TENNIS

can

tennis ball

player

shorts

GOOD LUCK!

player

skirt

wristbands

tennis court

post

net

service line

receiver

sideline

server

48

VOLLEYBALL

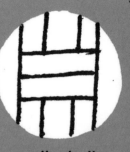

volleyball

block

spike

net

serve

spectacular dig

PHEW!

bump

headband

jersey

3

socks

set

knee pads

9

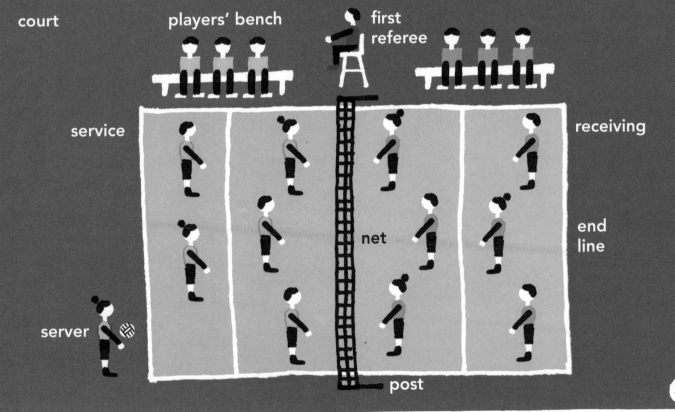

court

players' bench

first referee

service

receiving

net

end line

server

post

DESCRIPTION OF SPORTS

badminton
RACKET SPORT

Badminton is an individual or two-person team sport. Players hit the birdie over the net with a racket. A point is scored when the birdie lands on the opponent's side of the court.

baseball
BALL SPORT

Baseball involves two teams of nine players. The teams take turns at bat and in the field. To score a point, the batter must hit the ball and then run the bases, returning to home plate without being stopped by the other team.

basketball
BALL SPORT

Basketball involves two teams of five players. Players dribble or pass the ball down the court to score points by throwing or dunking the ball into their opponent's net.

cricket
BALL SPORT

Cricket involves two teams of eleven players. Like in baseball, the teams take turns at bat and in the field. To score points, the batter must hit the ball and then run between two wickets without being stopped by the other team.

cycling
CYCLING

A cycling road race is an individual or team competition. A race can take place on a single day or over several days. The first cyclist to finish the course wins.

diving
AQUATIC SPORT

Diving involves individuals or synchronized pairs. Competitors dive off a platform or springboard into a pool, executing a combination of specific positions. Points are earned for form, the difficulty of the routine and minimal splash.

fencing
COMBAT SPORT

Fencing is an individual or team sport, where two opponents are armed with weapons — an épée, a foil or a saber. Points are scored when the weapon touches specific places on an opponent's torso.

football
BALL SPORT

Football involves two teams of eleven players. Each team gets four chances to run at least ten yards with the ball before the ball is forfeited to the other team. To score points, the ball must be carried into or thrown (and caught) in the opponent's end zone or kicked between their goalposts.

golf
PRECISION SPORT

In golf, players use clubs to hit and sink the ball into holes on a 9- or 18-hole course, one hole at a time. The player who finishes the course using the fewest strokes wins.

gymnastics
GYMNASTICS

Gymnastics is an individual or team sport that includes different events performed on the floor or using an apparatus. Points are scored based on form, execution and the difficulty of the routine.

hockey
ICE SPORT

Ice hockey involves two teams of six players. To score points, players use sticks to move the puck down the ice and shoot it into their opponent's net. The goalies guard their teams' nets to block the puck from going in.

judo
COMBAT SPORT

In judo, a competitor uses different techniques to throw or pin her opponent to the ground. The match ends when a competitor earns ten points or when time runs out.

marathon
TRACK AND FIELD

In a marathon, competitors run a set route that is just over 42 km (26 mi.). The first runner to cross the finish line wins.

pole vault
TRACK AND FIELD

In pole vault, competitors use long poles to catapult themselves over a suspended horizontal bar. Each competitor has three chances to clear the bar. The winner must clear the bar at a greater height than his opponents.

riding

EQUESTRIAN SPORT

Riding is an individual or team sport, where the rider guides his horse through a set course. In jumping competitions, the horse must clear a series of obstacles along the course. Other competitions include dressage and combined eventing. Points are scored based on speed, form and the rider's control of the horse.

rowing

NAUTICAL SPORT

In rowing, individuals or teams (called crews) use oars to move their boats forward as quickly as possible over a set distance (2000 meters or 2187 yards in a sprint, or over several kilometers/miles in a head race).

sailing

NAUTICAL SPORT

In sailing, individuals or teams (called crews) race sailboats over a set distance. Courses vary in length, and can be as long as an ocean crossing. The fastest boat wins the race.

skiing

SNOW SPORT

Alpine skiing takes place on a snowy slope. In the giant slalom event, individual competitors must ski between several gates along the course. In the downhill event, they simply race down the slope. In both events, skiers race against the clock.

soccer

BALL SPORT

Soccer involves two teams of twelve players. To score points, players kick the ball down the field and try to shoot it into the opposing team's net without using their arms or hands. The goalies guard their teams' nets to block the ball from going in.

speed skating

ICE SPORT

Speed skating involves teams or individual skaters racing at the same time around an oval ice rink. The team or skater that finishes the course the fastest without interfering with the other competitors wins.

swimming

AQUATIC SPORT

Competitive swimming is an individual or team sport. Competitors must swim a set distance as quickly as possible using a certain stroke — the crawl, backstroke, breaststroke or butterfly.

tennis

RACKET SPORT

Tennis involves either two individual opponents or two-player teams. Using a racket, a player must hit the ball over the net onto her opponent's side of the court. A point is scored if the ball bounces more than once on the opponent's side of the court.

volleyball

BALL SPORT

Volleyball involves two teams of two or six players. Players must hit the ball over the net using their hands or forearms without letting the ball touch the ground. A point is scored when the ball lands on the opposing team's side of the court.

GLOSSARY

assault

In fencing, the assault is a friendly combat between two opponents.

coach

The coach is responsible for training athletes, both physically and mentally.

course

The course is the route and distance that competitors must complete.

defense

The defense, or defensive play, is when an individual or team tries to prevent their opponent from scoring. (The opposite of offense, or offensive play.)

drive

In rowing, the drive is the part of the stroke where the oar is pulled through the water to move the boat forward.

face-off

In a face-off in hockey, one player from each team tries to get possession of the puck when the referee drops it on the ice. The face-off signals the start of the game or period, or the restart of play after a goal is scored.

hajime

Hajime is a Japanese word that means "begin." It is used to signal the start of a judo match.

immobilization

In judo, immobilization is when a competitor is pinned to the ground by an opponent.

ippon seoi nage

Ippon seoi nage is a Japanese term used in judo for a one-arm shoulder throw.

kumi kata

Kumi kata is a Japanese term used in judo to describe a method of gripping one's opponent to gain an advantage in the match.

offense

The offense, or offensive play, is when an individual or team tries to score. (The opposite of defense, or defensive play.)

official

The official or referee makes sure that competitors follow the rules of the game.

opponent

An opponent is the individual or team one competes against.

peloton

In cycling, the peloton is the main group of competitors in a race. Riders save energy by biking together.

penalty

A penalty is given to a player for breaking a rule of the game.

red card

In soccer, the referee uses the red card to signal a penalty to a player who committed a serious offence. *See also* penalty *and* yellow card.

yellow card

In soccer, the referee uses the yellow card to signal a warning to a player. *See also* red card.

BIBLIOGRAPHY

Sources for English edition:

Fortin, François. *Sports: The Complete Visual Reference*. Willowdale, ON: Firefly Books, 2000.
Webster's Sports Dictionary. Springfield, MA: G&G Merriam Co., 1976.

Sources for original French edition:

Le dictionnaire visual. Montreal: Les Éditions Québec Amérique, 2014.
L'Encyclopédie visuelle des sports. Montreal: Les Éditions Québec Amérique, 2012.
Le grand dictionnaire terminologique. Québec: Office québécois de la langue française, 2012.

Answers to pages 24–25

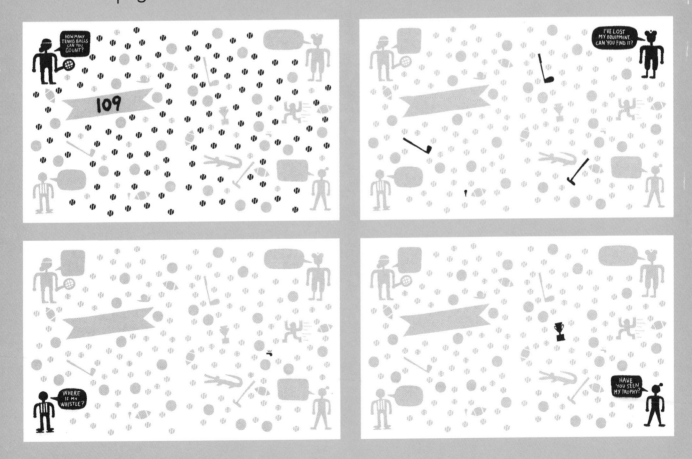

For Jules

Originally published in French under the title *Sport-O-Rama* by Comme des géants inc.

Kids Can Press acknowledges the financial support of the Government of Ontario, through the Ontario Media Development Corporation's Ontario Book Initiative.

Published in Canada by
Kids Can Press Ltd.
25 Dockside Drive
Toronto, ON M5A 0B5

Published in the U.S. by
Kids Can Press Ltd.
2250 Military Road
Tonawanda, NY 14150

www.kidscanpress.com

Original edition edited by Nadine Robert and Mathieu Lavoie
English edition edited by Katie Scott and Yvette Ghione
Designed by Mathieu Lavoie

Manufactured in Shenzhen, China, in 11/2014 through Asia Pacific Offset.

CM 15 0 9 8 7 6 5 4 3 2 1

Library and Archives Canada Cataloguing in Publication

Tardif, Benoit, 1983–
[Sport-o-rama. English]
    Sport-o-rama / written and illustrated by Benoit Tardif.

Translation of French book with same title.

ISBN 978-1-77138-327-1 (bound)

    1. Sports — Juvenile literature. I. Title. II. Title:
Sport-o-rama. English.

GV705.4.T3713 2015   j796   C2014-905040-2

Kids Can Press is a *l℗rUs*™ Entertainment company